Meelena

2016 Oganian

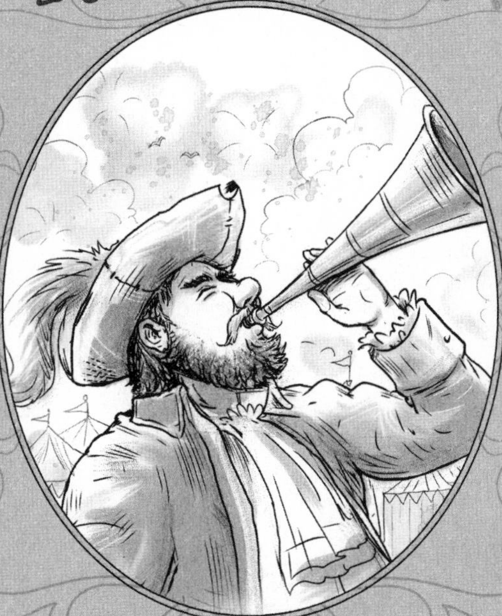

The Kingdom of Wrenly

7

Let the Games Begin!

By Jordan Quinn
Illustrated by Robert McPhillips

LITTLE SIMON

New York   London   Toronto   Sydney   New Delhi

LITTLE SIMON
An imprint of Simon & Schuster Children's Publishing Division
1230 Avenue of the Americas, New York, New York 10020
First Little Simon paperback edition March 2015
Copyright © 2015 by Simon & Schuster, Inc.
Also available in a Little Simon hardcover edition.
All rights reserved, including the right of reproduction in whole or in part in any form.
LITTLE SIMON is a registered trademark of Simon & Schuster, Inc., and associated colophon is a trademark of Simon & Schuster, Inc.
For information about special discounts for bulk purchases, please contact Simon & Schuster Special Sales at 1-866-506-1949 or business@simonandschuster.com.
The Simon & Schuster Speakers Bureau can bring authors to your live event. For more information or to book an event contact the Simon & Schuster Speakers Bureau at 1-866-248-3049 or visit our website at www.simonspeakers.com.
Cover and interior designed by Laura Roode
Manufactured in the United States of America 0215 FFG
2 4 6 8 10 9 7 5 3 1
Library of Congress Cataloging-in-Publication Data
Quinn, Jordan. Let the games begin! / by Jordan Quinn ; illustrated by Robert McPhillips. — First edition. pages cm. — (The kingdom of Wrenly ; 7)
Summary: As diverse subjects of Wrenly gather from far and wide to participate in the kingdom's Grand Tournament, a rude squire declares that girls cannot be knights, which makes Clara determined to prove that she can be anything she wants as long as she works hard enough for it.
ISBN 978-1-4814-2379-3 (pbk : alk. paper) — ISBN 978-1-4814-2380-9 (hc : alk. paper) — ISBN 978-1-4814-2381-6 (ebook) [1. Knights and knighthood—Fiction. 2. Sex role—Fiction. 3. Tournaments, Medieval—Fiction. 4. Princes—Fiction. 5. Kings, queens, rulers, etc.—Fiction. 6. Dragons—Fiction.] I. McPhillips, Robert, illustrator. II. Title.
PZ7.Q31945Let 2015
[Fic]—dc23
2014014827

CONTENTS

CHAPTER 1

The Grand Tournament

Prince Lucas and King Caleb stood on the balcony that overlooked the palace grounds. It was dawn, and hammers tapped, pulleys squeaked, and men called out orders. The mainland had become the setting for Wrenly's Grand Tournament.

The tournament took place once every two years. Everyone in the entire kingdom came to play in the

games and watch the shows. The big event was only a couple days away.

Lucas watched the preparations: The gardeners trimmed the hedge maze. The gnomes polished

the oversize marble chess pieces and chessboard. A squire slipped new covers over the archery targets. Villagers set up booths around the arena and stages.

Lucas turned to his father. "What do you love most about the Grand Tournament?" he asked.

"What I love most," said the king, "is the way the tournament brings together all the people and creatures in our kingdom."

"I like that too," said Lucas. "We get to see everyone's special skills and talents."

"Exactly," the king said. "And how about you? What do you like best about the Grand Tournament?"

Lucas's eyes grew wide. "I like the jousting and sword fighting."

Then Lucas pulled a sword from a scabbard on his belt. He had carved the sword from a piece of wood. Lucas showed off a few of his moves.

"I can't wait to show the Knight of Thornwood what I can do!" he said as he imitated a jab.

The Knight of Thornwood, also known as Sir Hugh, was the bravest knight in the kingdom.

The king laid his hand on Lucas's shoulder. "Do not grow up too fast, my little lion heart," he said.

"Can't stop me!" said Lucas as he squinted and faked a block. Then he stopped playing and looked up into his father's blue eyes. "Do you think Sir Hugh will give me some pointers?"

"I'm sure he will," said the king.

"Someday I'll fight with a real sword and a real lance, just like Sir Hugh!" Lucas said. "Ruskin and I will have grand adventures!" Ruskin

was Lucas's pet dragon. He was usually by Lucas's side, but for the last few days he'd been at Crestwood, training for the tournament. Now Ruskin was back on the mainland, but still hard at work practicing with the other dragons.

"And someday you'll be crowned a knight of Wrenly!" the king said.

Then Lucas held his sword so it pointed straight up.

"And I will defend the kingdom of Wrenly!" he declared.

CHAPTER 2

The Knight of Thornwood

Lucas climbed the arena's fence and sat on the highest rail. His friend Clara waved from on top of her horse, Scallop. Lucas waved back. Then he watched Clara put Scallop through her paces.

First they trotted around the arena. Then they cantered. And finally they galloped a lap. Clara pulled back on Scallop's reins and

trotted toward Lucas. The prince
yanked a carrot from his back
pocket. Scallop munched it from the
palm of his hand.

"You two make a great team,"
Lucas commented.

Clara patted Scallop and smiled.

"I'm thinking of entering the horse race at the Grand Tournament," she said.

"You should!" Lucas exclaimed.

"But it's all boys," Clara said.

"And when has that ever stopped you?" questioned Lucas.

Clara laughed. "True," she said.

"You should feel proud to be the only girl," said Lucas.

Clara liked that idea. Then she noticed something

unusual. "Where's Ruskin?" she asked. Lucas never went anywhere without him.

"He's up there!" said Lucas, pointing to the sky.

Clara saw the dragons of Crestwood soar overhead. Ruskin, the youngest and smallest dragon, led the way.

"He's been practicing for the tournament," Lucas said.

The dragons swooped into a loop de loop.

"Wow, Ruskin's gotten really good," said Clara.

"He's come a long way," agreed Lucas.

Then the arena's iron gate squeaked and swung open. A group of knights entered, followed by their squires. Each squire carried his knight's shield and led his horse.

Lucas gasped. "Look!" he cried. "It's the Knight of Thornwood! He wasn't supposed to arrive until tomorrow!"

"Who is he?" Clara asked.

"He's Sir Hugh, the bravest knight in the whole kingdom!" explained Lucas. "I've been to all his tournaments held at the castle. And I've read everything there is to know about him."

"Whoa," marveled Clara.

"I know," said Lucas. "My dream is to be just like him."

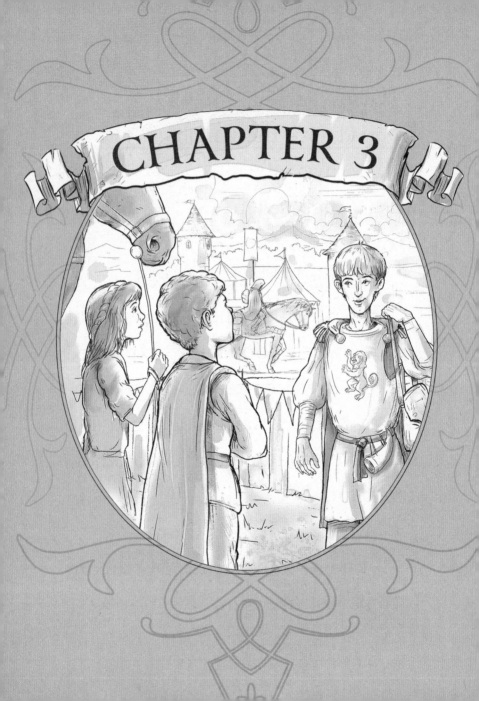

CHAPTER 3

A *Girl* Knight?

"They've spotted us!" said Lucas as he jumped down from the fence.

Clara slid out of her saddle and held Scallop by the bridle's reigns. "One of the squires is headed this way," she whispered.

Lucas brushed off his tunic and stood up straight.

A tall, skinny boy walked toward them. He had a picture of a lion

on his tunic—
the symbol of
the Knight of
Thornwood.
The squire bowed
before the prince.
"Good morning,
Your Highness," he
said. "My name is
Gilbert. I'm Sir Hugh's squire."

"Pleased to meet you, Gilbert,"
said Lucas. "You must be very
talented to serve Sir Hugh!"

"Yes, what a great honor!" Clara
added.

Gilbert paid no attention to Clara's comment. He kept his eyes on Lucas. It was as if Clara and Scallop weren't even there!

"Sir Hugh is a great teacher," Gilbert told Lucas. "Would you like me to introduce you?"

"Would I ever!" cried Lucas. "Sir Hugh is my all-time favorite hero."

"Mine too!" agreed Gilbert.

"Ahem," said Clara, trying to be part of the conversation. "Someday I hope to become a knight too!"

This got Gilbert's attention. He looked at her and laughed. Even Lucas looked surprised.

"Girls can't be knights!" declared Gilbert.

"And why not?" questioned Clara, folding her arms.

"Because all knights are *boys!*" argued Gilbert.

"That doesn't mean a girl can't be one!" Clara shot back.

"A *girl* knight?" said Gilbert. "Are you kidding?"

"No!" Clara said firmly. "I can be whatever I want—so long as I work hard enough for it."

Gilbert raised his arms in the air. "Who *is* this girl?" he cried.

Lucas grinned. "This is my friend

Clara Gills," he said proudly. "And to be fair, she would be a hard knight to beat."

Gilbert's eyes grew wide. Then he burst into laughter *again*. "That's very funny, Prince Lucas!" he said.

"But it wasn't actually a joke," said Lucas.

"Oh, I see," said Gilbert, controlling his laughter. "I'm so sorry." Then he went right back to ignoring Clara.

"Well, Your Highness, the knights are about to practice," he continued. "Would you like to stay and watch?"

"I'd love to!" Lucas exclaimed.

"Excuse me!" interrupted Clara. "But the arena is already booked."

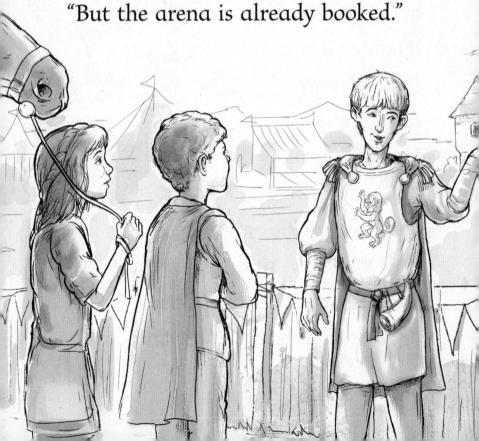

"What's *that* supposed to mean?" questioned Gilbert.

"It means I'm not done yet," said Clara.

"Knights overrule girls playing pony," said Gilbert.

"Then too bad for you!" said Clara, folding her arms. "You're only a squire."

Then Lucas gently pulled Clara to one side. "Be careful," he whispered. "He may not be a knight yet, but he's with the knights, and they do outrank you."

"Okay, fine!" Clara fumed. "I have better things to do, anyway."

Then she stormed out of the arena, with Scallop following close behind.

Combat Practice

In full armor, the Knight of Thornwood and the Knight of Briarwood, Sir Alwin, mounted their horses. They each took an opposite side of the arena.

They held up their lances—long wooden shafts with a blunt tip on the end. The flattened tips kept the knights from getting hurt. The first one to hit the opponent's shield or

helmet won. If they missed, they had to turn around and charge again.

Jousting showed off a knight's skills in horsemanship, his mastery of the lance, as well as his combat moves.

Lucas and Gilbert sat on the fence.
Gilbert untied a bugle from his belt
and offered it to Lucas. "Would you
like to start the match?" he asked.

"I'd love to!" Lucas replied, grasp-
ing the bugle.

He looked toward the knights. They nodded and lowered their lances into position. Lucas raised the bugle to his lips. Then he took a deep breath and blew. The knights charged at each other.

Sir Hugh struck. He swiftly jabbed Sir Alwin's shield and won the first round. Gilbert kept score by sliding beads across a wire. After five rounds Sir Hugh had

defeated Sir Alwin four to one.

"Now we're going to play Grab the Flag," Gilbert said.

He ran across the arena and joined the others on horseback. The knights and squires divided into two

teams. Each player wore a flag on his back. Sir Hugh's team wore blue flags, and Sir Alwin's team wore white. The first team to capture all the other team's flags won.

Lucas sounded the bugle.

The teams rushed toward each other. Round and round they galloped. Hooves pounded the dirt. The knights and squires cheered and hollered as they snatched the flags off one another's backs.

"Go, Gilbert!" shouted Lucas as he watched the squire yank a flag from another boy.

Gilbert waved the flag overhead. Then he galloped back into the fray. Sir Hugh plucked three flags in a row. His team won.

Gilbert trotted over to Lucas. "Now it's your turn," he said. "Follow me!"

Lucas jumped from the fence and followed Gilbert into the arena. The squires rolled a wooden horse into the ring. Then they set up a target at one end of the arena.

"I know you're a great horseman," said Gilbert. "But the wooden horse will help you get the

feel of holding a lance on horseback.
It's not as easy as it looks!"

Lucas nodded.

"Hop on!" said Gilbert.

Lucas climbed on top of the
wooden horse. Gilbert handed him

a lance. It felt heavy and awkward to Lucas. Gilbert showed him the proper way to tilt it.

"Now we'll pull you toward that target," said Gilbert, pointing. "When you get in range, aim the lance and hit the target."

"Got it!" said Lucas.

"Go for the bull's-eye!" Gilbert added.

Lucas nodded.

Gilbert and two other squires grabbed hold of the wooden horse's lead. Then they began to pull the horse. The wheels squeaked and the horse picked up speed.

As they neared the target, Lucas

held the lance steady. *Whack!* It struck the ring just outside the bull's-eye. The squires cheered.

"Good shot!" Gilbert shouted.

"Not bad for your first try!" said Sir Hugh, who had been watching. "You're a natural!"

"You sure are!" agreed Gilbert.

Lucas beamed. "May I try again?"

"Of course!" said Gilbert.

Lucas practiced with the lance all morning. Then he tried it from on top of a *real* horse.

"This is *so* hard," he said.

"It takes a lot of practice," said Sir Hugh.

"Then I will practice every day," vowed Lucas.

CHAPTER 5

At the Bakery

Lucas grabbed Ruskin from dragon training and raced to Clara's house. Clara lived above her father's bakery, the Daily Bread. Lucas couldn't wait to tell her about his morning. Bells jingled as Lucas pushed open the door to the bakery. Ruskin scampered in behind him.

"Well, look who's here!" said Clara's father, Owen Gills.

Mr. Gills reached into a basket and tossed a biscuit to Ruskin. Ruskin caught it between his teeth. Crumbs rained from his mouth as he munched the biscuit.

"It sure smells good in here!"
remarked Lucas.

"We're making cookies and bread
for the Grand Tournament," said
Clara. "You want to help?"

"Sure!" said Lucas. He loved to help in the bakery. Lucas washed his hands in a basin, took off his cape, and tied an apron around his waist.

"Look what we've made so far!" Clara said excitedly.

She pointed to racks of bread and cookies shaped like swords, shields, dragons, and horses. Lucas's stomach rumbled.

"I feel like I could eat a horse!" Lucas declared.

Mr. Gills laughed.

"Please, help yourself!" he said.

Lucas slid a horse-shaped cookie from a cookie tray and took a huge bite.

"*Mmm,*" he moaned. "Best horse I've ever had!"

"We only use the finest horses in our recipes," Mr. Gills said with a wink.

"Ew, that's disgusting!" said Clara as she plopped a ball of dough in front of Lucas.

Lucas began to roll the dough.

"You'll never guess what I did with the knights this morning," he said.

"What?" asked Clara.

"I rode a wooden horse and learned how to use a lance," Lucas said. "Sir Hugh even said I have natural talent!"

"That's a huge compliment, coming from the bravest knight in the land," Clara said with a smile.

"And Gilbert agreed with him," said Lucas.

Clara's face fell at the mention of the squire.

"I don't like Gilbert one bit," she said.

"I don't blame you," Lucas said. "He wasn't very nice to you."

"No kidding," agreed Clara.

"He just doesn't understand what kind of girl you are," Lucas said.

Clara stopped rolling her dough. "And just what

kind of girl *am* I?" she asked.

"You're strong, brave, and kind," he said, not missing a beat. "And you're a first-class horsewoman."

"Those are the qualities of a great knight!" declared Mr. Gills.

"Exactly," said Lucas.

CHAPTER 6

The Mermaids' Gift

"On guard!" shouted Clara.

Lucas and Clara dueled with two freshly baked cookie swords.

Clara swiped her sword across Lucas's blade. The tip of his sword broke off and landed on the floor. Ruskin gobbled it up.

"Touché!" Lucas cried.

Clara laughed.

Mr. Gills whistled through his

fingers. "No sword fights in the bakery," he said. "Take it outside. I have a lot of baking to do before the tournament."

"Sorry," Clara said. Then she turned to Lucas. "You want to go to Mermaid's Cove and make sand castles?"

"Sure!" answered Lucas.

They untied their aprons and ran out. Clara grabbed a bucket on the way. Ruskin squawked and raced after them. *Wham!* The door banged shut and the bells jangled harshly. Mr. Gills shook his head and chuckled.

"Race you!" shouted Clara.

They ran down the lane and onto the narrow path that led to the beach.

In a couple minutes, Clara was

out of breath. "You win!" she said.

They walked the rest of the way.

"What are you looking forward to at the tournament?" asked Clara.

"Jousting," said Lucas. "What about you?"

"The horse race," said Clara.

"Did you decide to sign up?" asked Lucas.

"I did!" said Clara. "After Gilbert made fun of me, I no longer minded being the only girl to race. Are you going to enter Ivan?"

"Can't," said Lucas. "Ivan threw a shoe. I can't ride him until he gets a new one, and all the blacksmiths are too busy with the tournament right now."

"That's too bad," Clara said.

"It stinks," said Lucas. "But at

least I'll get to watch you."

The friends jumped off a boulder and onto the beach. Then they walked along the water's edge. As they rounded the rocks into Mermaid's Cove, Clara gasped.

"Look!" she cried, pointing up ahead.

Lucas saw a large mound of sea-shells piled at the shore. They shimmered in the sun.

Clara and Lucas ran toward the shells.

"The mermaids left them!" exclaimed Clara. "This must be their gift for the tournament!"

The mermaids often left treasures

for Clara. They knew she loved to make seashell jewelry. Clara set her bucket on the sand. Together, Clara and Lucas filled it with beaded periwinkles, scallops, angel wings, spiral cone shells, and pink sand dollars.

"My bucket's already full!" Clara cried.

"I have an idea," said Lucas. He took off his cape and laid it on the beach. "Put some in here," he suggested.

They placed the rest of the shells on the cape, often stopping to admire the beauty of a shell as they worked. Then Lucas gently wrapped his cape around the delicate shells. He picked it up and it bulged like a sack of gold.

"We must have a thousand shells!" he exclaimed.

"I'll string them tonight," said Clara. Then we can hang shell garlands around the arena tomorrow."

Then they carefully walked back to Clara's with their treasures from the sea.

CHAPTER 7

Not *Him* Again!

Clara strung the mermaids' shells the rest of the day. The next morning she loaded her garlands into a wheelbarrow. Lucas steered the wheelbarrow to the blacksmith's shop and borrowed a hammer and nails. Then they rolled their decorations to the arena.

Lucas pounded the nails into the fence that surrounded the arena.

Clara draped the shell garlands from one nail to the next. She had enough strands to make it all the way around.

"How did the mermaids know exactly how many shells were needed?" said Clara in amazement.

"Because mermaids are magical," said someone behind them.

Clara and Lucas whirled around, and there stood Gilbert. He had come back with the knights for another practice. Clara frowned. *Oh no,* she thought. *Not HIM again.*

Gilbert bowed to Prince Lucas. Then he turned to Clara and began to clap as if she had just performed some kind of stunt.

"Well done!" he remarked. "I'm glad to see you've found an activity more fitting for a girl!"

Clara glared at Gilbert. "What's *that* supposed to mean?" she said.

Gilbert chuckled at Clara's response. "Calm down," he said. "I was trying to give you a compliment. Are you going to sell seashells at the tournament?"

"That's none of your business!" Clara said curtly.

She didn't want to admit to Gilbert that she liked anything girly.

"Clara makes the most beautiful seashell jewelry in the kingdom!" said Lucas proudly.

"I'm sure she does!" Gilbert exclaimed.

"Never mind that," said Clara. Then she challenged the squire. "Are you entering the horse race, Gilbert?"

"Of course," he replied.

"Well, *so am I!*" Clara declared.

Gilbert laughed so hard he snorted

like a pig. "That's the funniest thing I've ever heard!" he said.

"Why is that funny?" asked Clara, tapping one foot on the dirt.

"Because *girls* can't race!" Gilbert said matter-of-factly.

"That's what *you* think!" she exclaimed. Then she balled up her fists and marched away from the arena—again.

"Clara, wait!" called Lucas. "Come back!"

But Clara kept going.

"I'll show him!" she muttered as she stormed past the festival tents.

CHAPTER 8

Prove Yourself!

Flutes piped merrily as Lucas, Ruskin, and Clara entered the tournament at the King's Gate. The big day had finally arrived! Villagers, noblemen, fairies, trolls, gnomes, and wizards had all gathered for the festivities.

Lucas, Ruskin, and Clara walked to the bakery tent. Mr. Gills handed them each a sweet roll. They licked the icing on the way to the puppet

theater. Then they sat on a bale of
hay and watched a puppet show
about a princess and an evil queen.

There was so much to see at the
tournament! They saw acrobats,
potters, and glass blowers. They

sipped rainbow tea at the fairies' tea party. Then the children strolled to the fruits and vegetables tent. A troll juggled tomatoes.

Splat! A tomato landed on the troll's head.

Lucas laughed and pointed. "Hey, that's our friend Bren!" he cried.

Bren had helped Clara and Lucas find the vixberries

that had cured Ruskin of a terrible illness soon after he had hatched.

Bren's cheeks turned red when he saw his friends. He used the back of his hand to wipe the squished tomato from his face.

"When did you learn to juggle?" asked Clara.

Bren chuckled. "Last year," he

said. "Someday I hope to become a master juggler!"

"But I thought you were a farmer," said Lucas.

"I am," said Bren. "But I'd like to be a jester."

"Good for you!" declared Clara. "You can be anything you want, Bren—so long as you work hard enough for it!"

Then Bren smiled and picked out five apples from a nearby stand. He began to juggle them.

"That's exactly what I'm going to do," he said, keeping his eyes on the dancing fruit. "I'm going to prove myself!"

They watched Bren toss the fruit over and over. Then a bell rang in the distance. Clara counted the number of bells.

"It's time to get Scallop ready for the race!" she said excitedly. "It starts in an hour."

"I'll see you at the arena," Lucas said.

"Good luck!" added Bren.

Clara fixed her eyes on the boys.
"I'm going to prove myself too!" she
said firmly.

Then she turned and ran toward
the stables.

CHAPTER 9

Be Your Best

Lucas and Ruskin wandered the fairgrounds. They had a little time before Lucas would have to drop Ruskin off at the dragon pen.

They cheered on the gnomes in a tug-of-war match. Their friend Pilwinkle and his team tumbled to the ground as they pulled the other team over the line. After that Ruskin watched Lucas play a game of Jack

Straws, a gigantic version of pick-up sticks. Next they scampered toward the ice house.

"Remember when you melted the ice in the larder?" said Lucas, laughing.

Ruskin whimpered.

"We got in *so* much trouble!"

Then they stepped into the ice house. The cold air felt good. All around them stood the most beautiful ice sculptures Lucas had ever seen:

elephants, mammoths, mermaids, unicorns, knights, and dragons.

"Look, Ruskin!" cried Lucas. "The giants even made an ice sculpture of *us*!"

Lucas looked for someone to thank, but he knew the giants never stayed for the tournament. It was too warm for them near the castle so far beneath the icy mountains.

"Come on, Ruskin," said Lucas. "We need to get going!"

Lucas dropped Ruskin off at the dragon pen. Ruskin had to get ready for the dragon show. Then Lucas went to meet his parents at the fruits and vegetables tent. He spied them by the pumpkin display.

"I've never seen such large pumpkins in all of Wrenly!" commented Queen Tasha.

"We owe our beautiful crops to the Witch of Bogburp," said one of the trolls. He tipped his hat to Tilda the witch, who was standing nearby.

"She has definitely made up for the endless

rain she caused earlier," the troll went on. "Our soil has never been richer!"

"Well done!" said the king.

The witch blushed. Then she offered the king an apple from the fairies' apple orchard.

"My favorite!" said the king as he took a large bite.

The royal family sampled carrots, pears, cucumbers, and radishes. Then

they handed out ribbons for the
biggest and best-tasting fruits and
vegetables.

Soon the horns began to trum-
pet. The tournament was about to

begin! Lucas and his parents headed
for the grandstand.

"I'm sorry you and Ivan can't race
today," said the king.

"That's okay," said Lucas. "At least

I get to cheer on Clara and Gilbert."

The king smiled. "You're a good sport," he said.

"Thanks," said Lucas. "But the best part of the tournament is watching what others can do."

The king patted his son on the back. "That's what it's all about," agreed the king.

CHAPTER 10

The Big Race

"Hear ye! Hear ye! It's time for the tournament to begin!" shouted a herald to signal the start of the games. Then the dragons of Crestwood—red, green, purple, blue, and bronze—roared. The crowd looked up as the dragons flapped overhead in a V formation. Ruskin led the way.

The dragons swooped into loops, rolls, and spins—all in unison. They

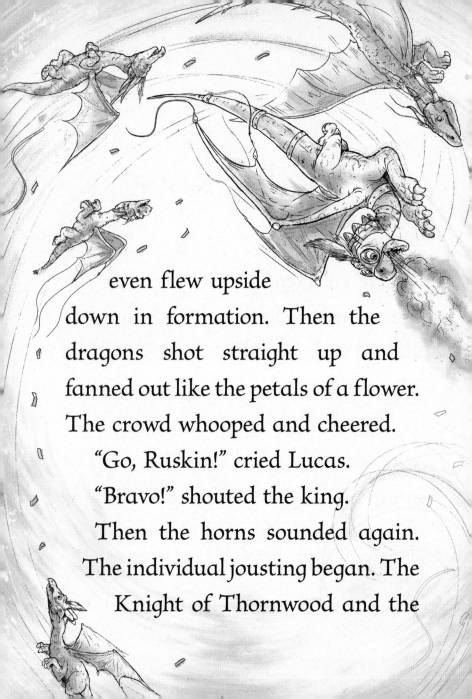

even flew upside
down in formation. Then the
dragons shot straight up and
fanned out like the petals of a flower.
The crowd whooped and cheered.

"Go, Ruskin!" cried Lucas.

"Bravo!" shouted the king.

Then the horns sounded again.
The individual jousting began. The
Knight of Thornwood and the

Knight of Briarwood paraded into the arena in bulky shining armor. They held their shields proudly.

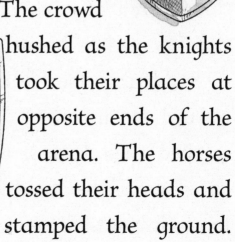

Sir Hugh had a lion on his shield. Sir Alwin wore a bear on his. The crowd hushed as the knights took their places at opposite ends of the arena. The horses tossed their heads and stamped the ground.

The knights sat stock-still on their steeds. They pointed their lances and peered at each other through the slits in their helmets.

Suddenly the horses charged toward each other. The knights gripped their lances. Hooves thundered across the arena. Lucas braced for the impact. Then—*whack!*—wood

splintered everywhere as Sir Hugh slammed his opponent's shield with his lance. Sir Alwin hit the ground with a clatter.

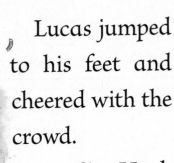

Lucas jumped to his feet and cheered with the crowd.

Sir Hugh took a victory lap. Then, like a gentleman, he helped Sir Alwin get up. Sir Alwin waved to the crowd to show he was unharmed. The crowd cheered even louder.

Someday I will be the best knight, Lucas thought.

Team jousting and sword fighting

followed. The squires played Grab the Flag, and Gilbert's team took first place.

Then it was time for the horse race. Lucas sat on his hands to keep from jumping out of his seat. The young horsemen as well as the lone horsewoman, Clara, lined up at the starting line.

"Clara's the only girl," remarked the king.

"That's right!" Lucas said proudly.

"Good for her!" said the queen.

Lucas spotted Gilbert. His horse was bigger and had longer legs than

Scallop. *He'll be tough to beat*, thought Lucas. Then the arena grew quiet. Gilbert folded his long legs close to his horse's sides. He flattened his lean frame along the horse's back. Clara did the same.

A herald blew the horn. Gilbert shot from the starting line. *Whoa,* thought Lucas. *He's fast!* Gilbert easily took the lead. Lucas kept his eyes on Clara and Scallop. They moved like one being. Gilbert and Clara left the other riders behind in a cloud of dust. They rode shoulder to shoulder as they thundered toward the finish line. The crowd roared as Clara crossed the line first.

"She *did* it!" Lucas shouted.

"She sure did!" exclaimed the queen.

"Wow!" cried the king, clapping.

People poured from the grand-stand and surrounded Clara. Her parents wriggled their way through the crowd to give their daughter a hug. Then Sir Hugh crowned Clara with a wreath of flowers.

"First place goes to Clara Gills!"
announced the knight.

The crowd clapped and cheered.
Lucas whistled.

"You must come train with me
when you're older," said Sir Hugh.

Clara's eyes filled with wonder. "I would be most honored!" she cried.

Then Gilbert held out his hand. "I was wrong about you, Clara," he said thoughtfully. "You've proven that you can do anything you set your mind to. You will make a fine knight."

Clara shook his hand and smiled. "Actually, I'm not really sure if I want to be a knight," she confessed.

Gilbert looked surprised. "You don't?"

"No," said Clara. "The armor looks too heavy and clunky."

King Caleb laughed. "It is!"

"Three cheers for Clara!" cried Lucas.

And everyone cheered in celebration.

Hear ye! Hear ye!
Presenting the next book from
The Kingdom of Wrenly!
Here's a sneak peek!

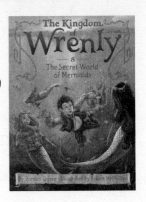

Prince Lucas and his best friend, Clara, swept dirt, leaves, and bits of straw into a corner of Ruskin's lair. They wanted the cave to be clean when Ruskin returned. Ruskin still had another week of training on the island of Crestwood. He was perfecting his fire breathing, and Grom had told Lucas that being around other dragons was good for him.

Excerpt from *The Secret World of Mermaids*

"Look at all the cobwebs!" cried Clara, pointing to the lair's corners.

"This place seems more like a home for spiders than for a dragon," agreed Lucas. "I can't wait until Ruskin can go on more adventures with us," the prince continued.

"Me too," agreed Clara. "I wonder what land we'll discover next."

"Well, wherever it is," answered Lucas, "*I'm* going to be the one to discover it!"

Clara stopped sweeping for a moment. "Why do you say it like *that*?"

Excerpt from *The Secret World of Mermaids*

Lucas shrugged. "I don't know. I guess it's because you always find everything first," said Lucas.

"I'm not trying to," Clara responded. "It's just because I know my way around the kingdom from all the bread deliveries I've done with my father."

"I know," said Lucas, "but I wish I could discover something before you just once."

"Well, don't worry," she said, pulling off a cobweb. "I know you'll uncover many mysteries before me. Just keep your eyes open."

Excerpt from *The Secret World of Mermaids*